# Jack and Z

Written by Jessica Ellis

Illustrated by Evelt Yanait

## Collins

# Jack is in bed.

Zain gets into bed too.

# Jack turns the light off.

Zain thinks of hugs with Mum.

Zain thinks of his kitten.

He thinks of food. Yum!

Zain sees the moon.

He hears the rain.

Zain turns to Jack.

# Zain feels better

# After reading

**Letters and Sounds:** Phase 3

**Word count:** 57

**Focus phonemes:** /ee/ /igh/ /oo/ /oo/ /ur/ /er/ /ai/ /ear/

**Common exception words:** the, he, of, to, I

**Curriculum links:** Understanding the World, People and Communities

**Early learning goals:** Reading: use phonic knowledge to decode regular words and read them aloud accurately; demonstrate understanding when talking with others about what they have read

## Developing fluency

- Encourage your child to sound talk and then blend the words, e.g. t/ur/n/s **turns**. It may help to point to each sound as your child reads.
- Then ask your child to reread the sentence to support fluency and understanding.
- Model reading the whole text to your child with expression.
- Practise reading the speech bubbles with expression and discuss how the children are feeling.

## Phonic practice

- Ask your child to sound talk and blend each of the following words: f/ee/l/s, l/igh/t, m/oo/n, r/ai/n, h/ear/s.
- Can your child think of any words that rhyme with **light**? (e.g. *sight, fright, bright, fight, might, tight, height*)

## Extending vocabulary

- Ask your child:
  - On page 5, Zain is feeling sad. What other words could you use to describe how Zain is feeling? (e.g. *unhappy, upset, miserable, tearful, scared, frightened*)
  - On page 7, Zain thinks of hugs with Mum. What other words can you use that mean hugs? (e.g. *cuddles*)

## Comprehension

- Turn to pages 14–15 and ask your child to retell you the story using each picture as a prompt. Can your child remember how Zain was feeling at each part of the story?